COLLECT THEM ALL!

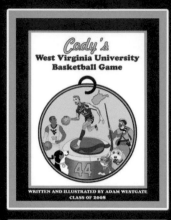

Cody's
West Virginia University
Basketball Game

WRITTEN AND ILLUSTRATED BY ADAM WESTGATE
CLASS OF 2008

Biscuit
Learns About Bullying

WRITTEN AND ILLUSTRATED BY ADAM WESTGATE

Officer Ruger
K-9 DETECTIVE

SERVICE WITH INTEGRITY

WRITTEN AND ILLUSTRATED BY ADAM WESTGATE

Cody the Shepherd's
West Point Tour

WRITTEN AND ILLUSTRATED BY ADAM WESTGATE

Cody the Shepherd's
Farm Adventure

WRITTEN AND ILLUSTRATED BY ADAM WESTGATE

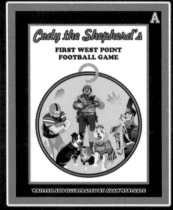

Cody the Shepherd's
FIRST WEST POINT
FOOTBALL GAME

WRITTEN AND ILLUSTRATED BY ADAM WESTGATE

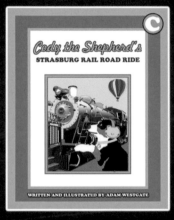

Cody the Shepherd's
STRASBURG RAIL ROAD RIDE

WRITTEN AND ILLUSTRATED BY ADAM WESTGATE

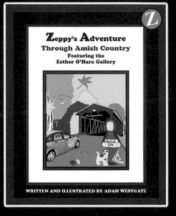

Zeppy's Adventure
Through Amish Country
Featuring the
Esther O'Hara Gallery

WRITTEN AND ILLUSTRATED BY ADAM WESTGATE

Paw Print Stories

**Inspiring, Educating,
and Bringing Joy to Young Readers**

Morgantown, West Virginia

For children who love dogs and West Virginia University basketball!

www.mascotbooks.com

Cody's West Virginia University Basketball Game

For more information, please contact:
Mascot Books
560 Herndon Parkway #120
Herndon, VA 20170
info@mascotbooks.com

CPSIA Code: PRT0916A
ISBN-13: 978-1-63177-414-0

Printed in the United States

Cody's
West Virginia University
Basketball Game

WRITTEN AND ILLUSTRATED BY ADAM WESTGATE

CLASS OF 2008

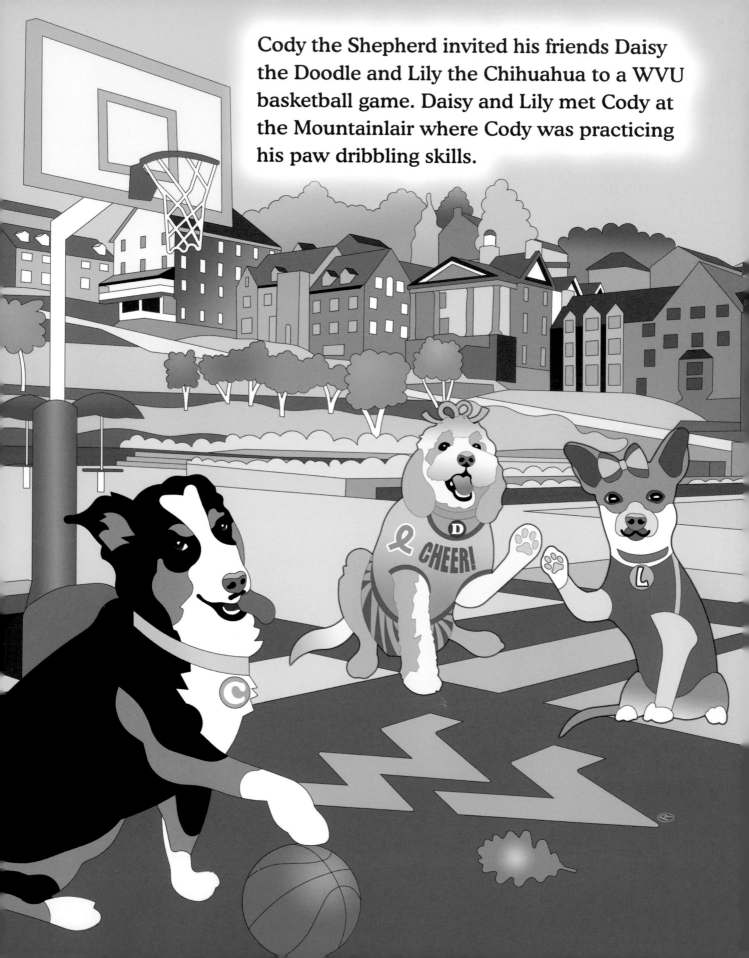

Cody the Shepherd invited his friends Daisy the Doodle and Lily the Chihuahua to a WVU basketball game. Daisy and Lily met Cody at the Mountainlair where Cody was practicing his paw dribbling skills.

Cody showed the Mountainlair to Daisy and Lily.

Cody said, "One of the coolest things about the Mountainlair is the flags from all over the world. WVU is proud to have talented students from all of these countries study here. Can you find the American flag?"

Daisy looked up and barked.

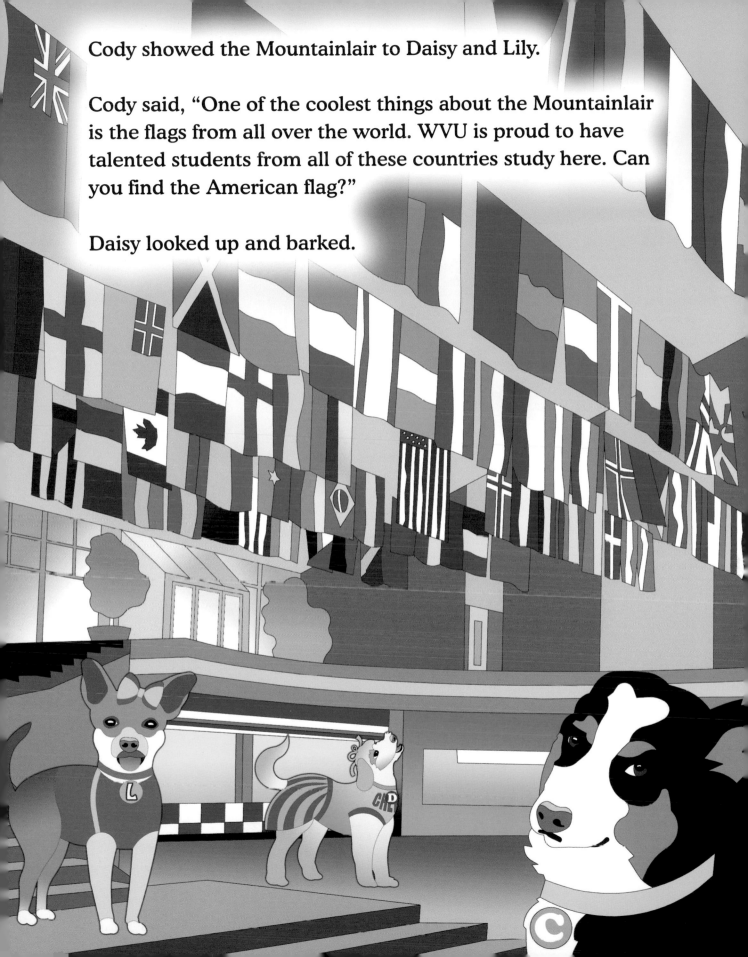

Near the Mountainlair was the Personal Rapid Transit or PRT. Cody, Daisy, and Lily sat by the front window for the best view while they rode the PRT to the basketball arena, called the Coliseum. The West Virginia University mascot, the Mountaineer, was also on his way to the Coliseum for the game!

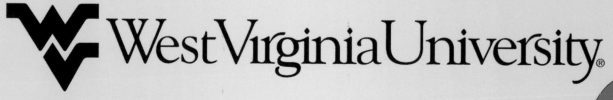

At the Coliseum, fans played games, ate delicious food, and talked about their favorite players. The Mountaineer thanked all the fans for supporting the team and posed for pictures.

"Did you know the Coliseum is also used for other sporting events, concerts, and graduation?" asked the Mountaineer.

At one of the tailgates, a little girl named Sarah played a game called ring toss. "Tailgating is a great way to have fun and show school spirit, and WVU fans are some of the best at it in the country," said Cody.

LET'S GO!™

Cody wanted to play too! He noticed a ring on the ground near his paws, picked it up, and placed it over a peg. Sarah showed her WVU spirit by clapping for him.

Cody showed Daisy and Lily the Jerry West statue in front of the Coliseum.

"Jerry West played at WVU and is one of the most well-known players in the history of basketball," said Cody. "He won both an NBA title and an Olympic gold medal after playing at WVU."

Cody borrowed a fan's basketball and posed just like the Jerry West statue. Sarah from the ring toss game cheered for him.

Cody, Daisy, and Lily arrived at their seats and were excited for the game to start. The Coliseum looked like a sea of gold and blue!

Soon after the game started, a WVU player soared through the air for a dunk. The crowd roared.

The WVU cheerleaders wore special uniforms and held gold and blue pom poms. They worked hard to encourage the team and entertain the crowd. The cheerleaders noticed Daisy in the stands and invited her to lead them in a cheer.

Musket, the Mountaineer's friend, had a special job at halftime. He used a slingshot to shoot rolled up t-shirts to cheering WVU fans. The Mountaineer helped Musket aim by pointing high in the stands. Musket let the t-shirt fly.

Cody was in for a surprise. The
t-shirt flew right in his direction.
Cody jumped into the air and caught
it with his paws.

Cody felt very proud with his new WVU t-shirt on. The WVU team was losing near the end of the game but Daisy had a plan to help. Daisy pointed at Cody who used a "Let's Go" megaphone. Next Daisy pointed at Lily who used a "Mountaineers" megaphone. Soon fans all over the stadium were chanting, "Let's Go Mountaineers," which energized the team.

The WVU pep band played "Take Me Home, Country Roads" as the clock wound down for one last play. The Mountaineers were losing by one point so a basket would win the game.

The WVU point guard brought the ball up the court. He passed the ball to his open teammate with only a few seconds to go.

The WVU player caught the pass and jumped straight up in the air to shoot the ball towards the basket. The game clock buzzed just after the ball left his hands.

The crowd gasped as the basketball rolled around the rim. It looked like the basketball would fall without going through the hoop, so Cody, Daisy, and Lily blew as hard as they could towards the basket.

The basketball fell through the hoop with a SWOOSH sound. WVU had won! Cody, Daisy, and Lily had done their part to help the team. Win or lose, they cheered, clapped, and supported the team.

After the game, Cody bought a brand new WVU basketball. That night at home, Cody fell asleep with one paw on his new basketball. His favorite poster was on the wall behind him.

The End

The Jerry West Statue at the WVU® Coliseum

Top: The author at a reading of his book, *Officer Ruger K-9 Detective*. Proceeds from sales of this book benefited Concerns of Police Survivors, a charity that supports the families of fallen law enforcement officers.

Bottom: Adam's loyal and loving dog Cody. Adam's sister's dog Daisy, shown on the next page, also stars in many *Paw Print Stories*.

Left:
Adam with Cody

Right:
Daisy The Doodle

About the Author

Adam Westgate was born in Lancaster, Pennsylvania in 1984. He earned his B.S. degree in Landscape Architecture from West Virginia University and has worked as a professional landscape designer and correctional officer. Adam began his literary career by writing and illustrating a book for his niece. His love of animals was instilled at an early age through caring for family pets. At the beginning of 2015, Adam launched his book series, *Paw Print Stories,* by writing children's books featuring several dog characters. Adam hopes to inspire children, share his stories with the world, and support great causes.

Please stay in touch and get the latest updates on the *Paw Print Stories* Facebook page. Please send your comments about the book to:

Adam.PawPrintStories@gmail.com
Website: PawPrintStories.com

Paw Print Stories offers custom books for colleges, school districts, businesses, charity work, and fundraising projects. Books are available on Amazon.com or by contacting *Paw Print Stories* directly.

Pink ribbons are displayed throughout the
book to promote breast cancer awareness.
Thank you for reading!